It's the coolest sch

Young Teggs Stegosaur is a pupil at **Astrosaurs ACADEMY** – where dinosaurs to be space-exploring **Astrosaurs**. h his best friends Blink and Dutch side him, amazing adventures and far-out fun are never far away!

Collect all the **Astrosaurs ACADEMY** books. Free collector cards in every one or you to swap with your friends.

or more astro-fun visit the website
www.astrosaursacademy.co.uk

LIBRARIES

www.**kidsatrandomhouse**.co.uk

I2553107

Read all the adventures of Teggs, Blink and Dutch!

DESTINATION: DANGER!
CONTEST CARNAGE!

Read Teggs's adventures as a real ASTROSAUR!

RIDDLE OF THE RAPTORS
THE HATCHING HORROR
THE SEAS OF DOOM
THE MIND-SWAP MENACE
THE SKIES OF FEAR
THE SPACE GHOSTS
DAY OF THE DINO-DROIDS
THE TERROR-BIRD TRAP
THE PLANET OF PERIL
TEETH OF THE T. REX
specially published for World Book Day
THE STAR PIRATES
THE CLAWS OF CHRISTMAS
THE SUN-SNATCHERS

Find out more at www.astrosaurs.co.uk

Astrosaurs ACADEMY

STEVE COLE

CONTEST CARNAGE!

Illustrated by Woody Fox

RED FOX

CONTEST CARNAGE!
A RED FOX BOOK 978 1 862 30555 7

First published in Great Britain by Red Fox,
an imprint of Random House Children's Books
A Random House Group Company

This edition published 2008

3 5 7 9 10 8 6 4 2

Copyright © Steve Cole, 2008
Cover Illustration, map and cards © Dynamo Design, 2008
Illustrations copyright © Woody Fox, 2008

The right of Steve Cole to be identified as the author of this work has been asserted in
accordance with the Copyright, Designs and Patents Act 1988.

All rights reserved. No part of this publication may be reproduced, stored in
a retrieval system, or transmitted in any form or by any means, electronic, mechanical,
photocopying, recording or otherwise, without the prior permission of the publishers.

The Random House Group Limited supports the Forest Stewardship Council (FSC),
the leading international forest certification organization. All our titles that are printed on
Greenpeace-approved FSC-certified paper carry the FSC logo. Our paper procurement
policy can be found at www.rbooks.co.uk/environment.

Mixed Sources
Product group from well-managed
forests and other controlled sources
www.fsc.org Cert no. TT-COC-2139
© 1996 Forest Stewardship Council

Set in 16pt Bembo

Red Fox Books are published by Random House Children's Books,
61–63 Uxbridge Road, London W5 5SA

www.**kids**at**randomhouse**.co.uk
www.**rbooks**.co.uk

Addresses for companies within The Random House Group Limited can be found at:
www.randomhouse.co.uk/offices.htm

THE RANDOM HOUSE GROUP Limited Reg. No. 954009

A CIP catalogue record for this book is available from the British Library.

Printed in the UK by CPI Bookmarque, Croydon, CR0 4TD

For Annie Eaton

WELCOME TO THE COOLEST SCHOOL IN SPACE . . .

Most people think that dinosaurs are extinct. Most people believe that these weird and wondrous reptiles were wiped out when a massive space rock smashed into the Earth, 65 million years ago.

HA! What do *they* know? The dinosaurs were way cleverer than anyone thought . . .

This is what *really* happened: they saw that big lump of space rock coming, and when it became clear that dino-life could not survive such a terrible crash, the dinosaurs all took off in huge, dung-powered spaceships before the rock hit.

They set their sights on the stars and left the Earth, never to return . . .

Now, 65 million years later, both plant-eaters and meat-eaters have built massive empires in space. But the carnivores are never happy unless they're causing trouble. That's why the Dinosaur Space Service needs herbivore heroes to defend the

Vegetarian Sector. Such heroes have a special name. They are called ASTROSAURS.

But you can't change from a dinosaur to an astrosaur overnight. It takes years of training on the special planet of Astro Prime in a *very* special place . . . the Astrosaurs Academy! It's a sensational

space school where
manic missions
and incredible
adventures are
the only
subjects! The
academy's doors
are always open,
but only to the
bravest, boldest
dinosaurs . . .

And to YOU!

*NOTE: One of the most famous astrosaurs of
all is Captain Teggs Stegosaur. This staggering
stegosaurus is the star of many stories . . . But
before he became a spaceship captain, he was a
cadet at Astrosaurs Academy. These are the
adventures of the young Teggs and his friends
— adventures that made him the dinosaur he
is today!*

Talking Dinosaur!

How to say the prehistoric names in
CONTEST CARNAGE!

SEISMOSAURUS – *SIZE-moh-SORE-us*

DIPLODOCUS – *di-PLOH-de-kus*

DICERATOPS – *dye-SERRA-tops*

ANKYLOSAUR – *an-KILE-oh-SORE*

DRYOSAURUS – *DRY-oh-SORE-us*

PTERODACTYL – *teh-roh-DACT-il*

BAROSAURUS – *bar-oh-SORE-us*

TRICERATOPS – *try-SERRA-tops*

SAUROPELTA – *SORE-oh-PEL-ta*

KENTROSAURUS – *KEN-troh-SORE-us*

IGUANODON – *ig-WA-noh-don*

STEGOSAURUS – *STEG-oh-SORE-us*

HADROSAUR – *HAD-roh-sore*

CARNOTAUR – *kar-noh-TORE*

The cadets

THE DARING DINOS

Teggs   Dutch   Blink

DAMONA'S DARLINGS

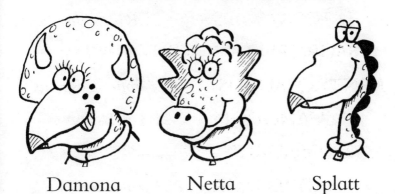

Damona   Netta   Splatt

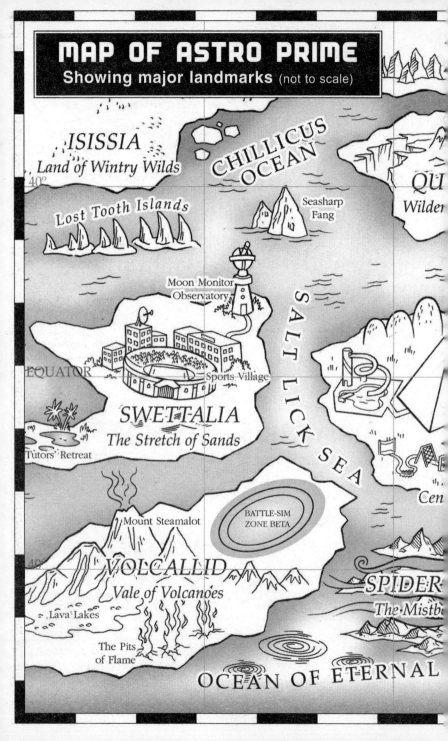

Chapter One

THE MEGASAUR CHALLENGE

"Sit down, shut up and listen!" roared Commander Gruff.

Young Teggs Stegosaur and his classmates did as they were told. When fifty tons of scary seismosaurus shouted at you, it wasn't wise to disobey. Especially as Gruff was headteacher at Astrosaurs Academy!

"Remember, cadets," Gruff went on, a green banana clamped in his mouth like a cigar. "If you do well and pass all your missions here, you will each join the ranks of the Dinosaur Space Service – and become an astrosaur!"

Teggs felt a shiver of excitement. All his life he had dreamed of going on exciting adventures in space, fighting evil and protecting the innocent. And now he had joined the Astrosaurs Academy on the planet Astro Prime, he was closer to making those dreams come true!

The academy was like a special school built in the middle of a super-cool adventure park. There were playing fields, a giant swimming pool, an assault course, an athletics track . . . even a special ski slope! All the astrosaur cadets lived in the special dino-dorms nearby, close to the enormous launch pads for visiting spaceships. Teggs loved to lie awake at night, listening to the astro-jets land and take off again. One day he hoped to be flying such ships himself.

"Pay attention, Teggs!" Gruff snapped, glowering down at him. "No daydreaming in class."

Teggs shook his head. "No, sir! Sorry, sir!"

Gruff nodded, chomping on the unripe banana. "Now, before we start today's lesson on how to read star charts, I have some news. A brand-new contest is about to take place, right here on Astro Prime. It is called the 'Megasaur Challenge'!"

A buzz of excitement went round the classroom. Teggs glanced at his best friends beside him, Dutch and Blink.

Dutch Delaney was a sporty diplodocus – small, dark green, plucky and happy-go-lucky – while Blink Fingawing was a bright, bespectacled, yellow dino-bird with a mind as sharp as his beak. Both of them were smiling.

"A contest!" whispered Dutch. "That's like, totally awesome!"

"You don't know what sort of contest it is yet," Blink pointed out.

Dutch shrugged. "Any contest is a good contest, dude."

"What about a pants-washing contest?" Teggs said, and they all burst out laughing.

"All right, you lot, that's enough," growled Commander Gruff. "The Megasaur Challenge is a contest of strength and skill. The organizers hope that plant-eating dinosaurs from all over space will enter it next year. But first they want to test out the challenges — on *you*."

"Wow!" said Blink, blinking quickly. "You mean, they can find out if the events are too easy or too hard by seeing how we do?"

"That's right, cadet," said Gruff. "And it means the first ever Megasaur could be someone in this room!"

5

"It's *me*!" cried a pretty red diceratops in the front row. "Damona Furst – the Megasaur . . . I can just hear the judge saying it."

Dutch pulled a face. "I can just hear me being sick!"

"You always think you're best, Damona," said Blink.

"That's because I *am*, beak-features!" She put her nose in the air. "I bet I find *all* the events completely easy."

"I wouldn't be too sure of that," Gruff warned her. "Cadets in the years above you are also taking part, so it will be a tough contest."

"Sounds cool!" said Teggs. "Where will this Megasaur Challenge be held?"

"In the academy's special sports village in the continent of Swettalia," Gruff explained. "The first round begins tonight! How many of you want to take part?"

All thirty dinosaurs in the class put up their hands and claws.

"Good!" boomed Gruff. "An astro-jet will take you there at lunch time."

"Er, one more thing, sir," said Teggs. "Do we compete by ourselves or in teams?" Cadets at Astrosaurs Academy usually worked in teams of three – Teggs, Blink and Dutch had made a team called the Daring Dinos.

"You will each enter the contest separately," said Gruff. "However, every point you score will add to a grand total for your usual teams. The team with the highest score will win a special medal."

Blink blinked madly at Teggs and Dutch. "Imagine if we win it!"

"Dream on!" said Damona. She grinned at her own team-mates – a pink ankylosaur called Netta and a sleek, green dryosaurus named Splatt. "Damona's Darlings will win for sure."

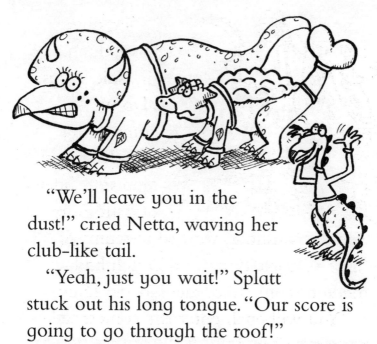

"We'll leave you in the dust!" cried Netta, waving her club-like tail.

"Yeah, just you wait!" Splatt stuck out his long tongue. "Our score is going to go through the roof!"

"You'll follow it if you don't shut up!" said Dutch hotly.

"Save your energy for the Megasaur Challenge, cadets," rumbled Gruff with a little smile. "One thing's for sure – you are going to need it!"

Chapter Two

THE CHALLENGE BEGINS

Teggs found it hard to concentrate on
his lessons after that. He couldn't wait
for lunch time to come!

As soon as the bell went, all the cadets
zoomed off to the
dino-dorms to
pack. Half an hour
later, they were
squashed into the
astro-jet as it took off
into the clear blue skies.

Teggs watched from the window as
rolling blue hills made way for
shimmering orange oceans. Before long,
sandy yellow deserts came into sight as

they flew over the warm continent of
Swettalia.

Minutes later, Teggs spotted the sports
village far below – a giant square of
concrete and metal rising up from the
sand. In the middle was a huge white
stadium filled with neatly-nibbled grass.
A large crowd had gathered there
already! And as the astro-jet came into
land, Teggs could see many other
buildings huddled around it – changing
rooms, hotels, a TV station, even a
special hospital.

The moment the jet doors opened, Teggs and his friends burst outside in excitement. The sun was shining and the air was fresh. Flying taxis – carriages towed by large pterodactyls – were lined up to take the cadets onwards.

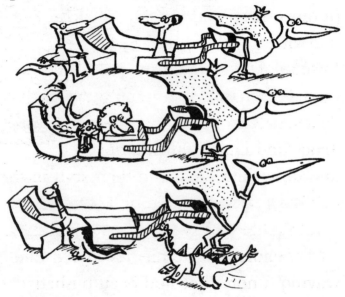

"Next stop, the five-star Ferns Hotel," said Damona grandly, climbing carefully into her carriage with Netta and Splatt.

"Awesome!" yelled Dutch. He, Teggs and Blink bundled inside their own taxi. "Quick, driver – get flapping!"

It was only a short ride to the smart hotel. The rooms were huge and full of tasty trees and vines. Instead of carpets they had delicious long grass! Teggs and Dutch quickly ate and unpacked, chucking their stuff in the first drawers they could find, while Blink neatly folded his sports kit and pyjamas.

"Let's hurry downstairs," twittered Blink, waving a note that had been pushed under the door. "The organizers want to welcome us all to the Challenge!"

"Before we go . . ." Teggs looked at his friends. "Guys, we are here to take part in a big contest – not as dinosaurs but as *Megasaurs*. Do we dare?"

Blink and Dutch put their hands on top of Teggs's. "WE DARE!" they all shouted, and ran whooping from the room.

The Daring Dinos found a crowd of cadets in the hotel lobby. They had gathered in front of a big barosaurus in a blue suit.

"Welcome to Swettalia for the very first Megasaur Challenge!" the barosaurus said. "My name is Mr Edvill and I am the organizer. I am very pleased to see so many contestants, and so is my chief trainer, Bomp."

Bomp nodded quickly. He was a chunky triceratops in black shorts and a green vest. "Some of the older astrosaur cadets are already here, ready to take part. And the DSS has kindly allowed sponsors and spectators from all over the Vegetarian Sector to come and watch."

Teggs gulped. It sounded like there would be quite an audience to cheer them on!

"As the youngest dinosaurs taking part, you will start off the challenge," Mr Edvill explained. "Your names are listed on a notice board outside the hotel, along with the start time of your events. Good luck!"

"*Gangway*," shouted Splatt, sprinting off to see.

Teggs raced after him, leading a dinosaur stampede that shook the ground! Mr Edvill waved them off while Bomp ran after them. Blink, meanwhile, flew over all their heads and reached the notice board first. The other cadets crowded around him.

"Our first event is robot boxing," Blink reported.

Dutch stretched his neck to look at the list. "Teggs, our boxing matches start in just an hour!"

"So does mine," Damona realized. "And yours, Netta!"

"Yay!" Netta thumped her tail on the ground in excitement.

Blink sighed. "Mine is after yours."

"You can cheer us on," Teggs suggested. "And then we will cheer *you* on."

"Jump in the flying taxis, you lot," Bomp urged them. "It's time to take the Megasaur Challenge!"

One lot of taxis took cadets to join the crowds in the stadium. The other took the first contestants to get ready for their event.

Teggs and Dutch went through to the boys' changing rooms with three other dinosaurs and collected their special Megasaur sports kits. Boxing gloves of all sizes had been left out for them too. Teggs put one glove on each hand and another on his tail, and Dutch did the same.

"Time to box a robot's butt!" said
Teggs.

Feeling excited but also very nervous,
he led the way out into the sunlit, grassy
arena. Damona, Netta
and three other
girl-dinos left
their changing
rooms at the same
time. They wore
pink sparkly boxing
gloves and matching
ribbons around their tails.

The audience waved and cheered for
them all from the stands. Teggs could see
Blink, Splatt and lots of their friends
jumping about and whooping. But as he
stared around the stadium he could see
no sign of where they would be fighting
– or what.

"Presenting the first event!" Mr Edvill's
voice echoed over the stadium speakers.
"Robo-Boxing Action!"

Bomp jogged over to them and clicked a button on a remote control. Suddenly, ten huge squares opened up in the grassy floor . . . and with a clank and a rattle, ten boxing rings rose up from under the ground to fill the space! In the middle of each ring sat a metal cube the size of a washing machine.

"To win, you must punch the cube three times," Bomp explained. "Off you go!"

"We have to box with a *box*?" said Teggs. He had been expecting a massive monster with steel muscles and fists like suitcases. Swapping baffled looks with his fellow cadets, Teggs shrugged and ran off to a ring.

"Go, dinos, go!" The cheers and shouts rang out all around. The noise was deafening! Teggs's heart began to race. Stay cool, he thought. How hard can it be to beat a box?

Teggs picked a ring and climbed

under the ropes. But the moment he did, ten long, mechanical tentacles uncurled from inside the cube – each with a huge boxing glove on the end! The gloves twitched in the air, as if the robot was somehow sniffing him out.

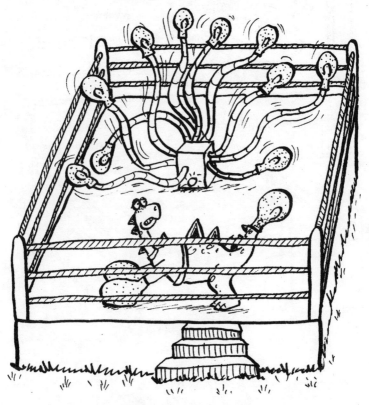

He looked nervously at his friends' rings. The same thing had happened.

"Er, Teggs?" Dutch yelled from the ring beside his, as the robots' arms  swayed like massive metal cobras. "I think we're in trouble!"

Bomp rang a bell.

"Round one!" yelled Mr Edvill.

Teggs gulped as ten robotic fists came hurtling towards him . . .

Chapter Three

A RED ALERT

Teggs dived away from the flailing
tentacles. He heard the robot's fists
whistle past his ears and whack the
ropes. He tried to scurry round behind
the box, but the mechanical arms
were already whipping back
to get him.

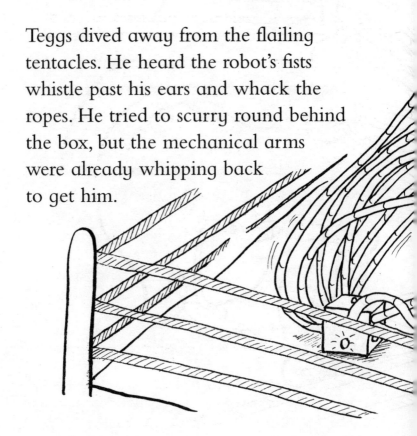

"*Whoa!*" shouted Teggs. He blocked five fists with his tail, but the other five were heading straight for his face. He raised up his two front legs and beat the blows away.

WHACK!
"Oof!"
THUMP!

Teggs glanced to his left and saw a pink dinosaur fly through the air and land on the grass in a daze. It was Netta. Her robot had knocked her right out of the ring!

The crowd gasped and booed.

And already Teggs's robot was preparing to strike again. Eight tentacles lashed out towards him. Teggs ducked another blow and looked right to see how Dutch was doing. The robot's fists were flying, and Dutch was dancing about from side to side so he made a harder target.

But then, Teggs got a boxing glove in
the snout and another in his belly. He
gasped as five more blows sent him
tumbling back against the ropes . . . and
then *another* five, landing faster and
harder. Suddenly, he found himself
squashed on his side, being dragged by
his legs back and forth across the
canvas . . .

"This thing's mopping the floor with
me," Teggs groaned. "Literally!"

Teggs kicked with all his strength to break the robot's grip. Then he kept his tummy flat against the floor but stretched his tail high up in the air as a target. The robot whacked it hard with its many fists, again and again. Teggs gasped as the boxing glove was knocked from the tip of his tail. But all the time he was wriggling forward, closer to the cube. He could see a red light flashing at its base . . .

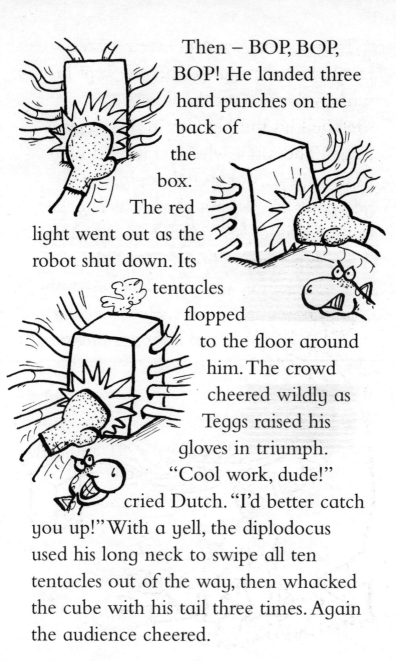

Then – BOP, BOP, BOP! He landed three hard punches on the back of the box. The red light went out as the robot shut down. Its tentacles flopped to the floor around him. The crowd cheered wildly as Teggs raised his gloves in triumph.

"Cool work, dude!" cried Dutch. "I'd better catch you up!" With a yell, the diplodocus used his long neck to swipe all ten tentacles out of the way, then whacked the cube with his tail three times. Again the audience cheered.

And a moment later they roared yet
again as Damona put an extra boxing
glove on her nose horns and charged
through the thrashing tentacles to crash
into the cube. She hit it twice more with
her front legs. *KA-BLAMMMM!* It went
up in smoke, hiding Teggs's view of the
other contestants.

Then Mr Edvill's voice echoed out of
the stadium's speakers. "And so, the
results!" he cried. "Six cadets have lost
out . . . but Teggs, Dutch, Damona and
Akk stay in the Megasaur Challenge!"

"Wheeee!" Akk – a black sauropelta –
burst out of the smoke and started a
victory lap around the stadium.

Damona and Dutch followed her, while
Teggs went to check Netta was all right.

"Well done, Teggs." She sighed, sitting
on the grass while one of the trainers
looked at her ankle. "Those dumb robots
pack a real wallop. I hurt my leg."

"I didn't think the first round would
be so tough," Teggs admitted. He turned
to a burly kentrosaurus security guard
standing nearby.

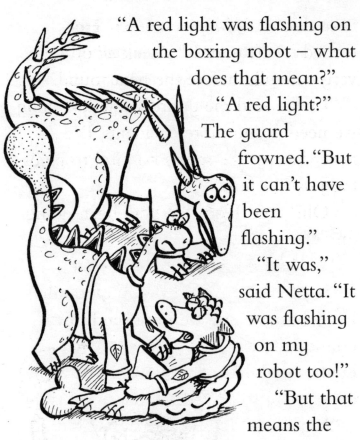

"A red light was flashing on the boxing robot – what does that mean?"

"A red light?" The guard frowned. "But it can't have been flashing."

"It was," said Netta. "It was flashing on my robot too!"

"But that means the robo-boxer was set to 'Super smash and squish' mode instead of 'Beginners'." The guard looked horrified. "It might have punched you to pieces!"

"These robo-boxers must be faulty," said Bomp, who had come to see what was wrong. "I set them myself only an hour ago and they were fine!" He turned to the guard. "Check *all* of them very carefully before the next round."

"I will," said the guard. "The last thing we need is any more accidents. I've never known the sports hospital to be as busy as it is now!"

"Oh?" said Teggs. "What's been going on?"

"We had a lot of bad luck while setting things up," said Bomp gloomily. "Still, busy or not, we must send this young lady to the hospital at once."

"My ankle isn't that bad!" said Netta.

"Better to be safe than sorry," Bomp insisted. "I'll fetch a stretcher."

As Bomp went off, Teggs noticed a cleaning dinosaur in a white coat hovering nearby – a blue skinned edmontonia. But he wasn't cleaning. He was staring at the faulty robot Teggs had beaten.

Then Damona, Dutch and Akk came running up.

"Netta," Damona cried. "Are you OK?"

"Yeah, what happened?" Dutch asked.

"You could call it a *red* alert!" Teggs looked at his friends. "Did any of you see red lights on your robots?"

Dutch and Akk shook their heads, but

Damona nodded. "Yes! The harder it hit me, the more the red light flashed."

"Another faulty robot!" The security guard walked away, shaking his head. "However could this have happened?"

"Perhaps someone made the robots go wrong on purpose," said Teggs slowly.

Netta gasped. "Who would want to do that?"

"I don't know," Teggs admitted. He saw the cleaner staring at him, and lowered his voice. "But I have the feeling something strange is going on around here . . . and I'm going to get to the bottom of it!"

Chapter Four

ACCIDENTS ON PURPOSE?

Netta was taken to the sports hospital.
Damona went with her. Meanwhile,
Teggs, Dutch and Akk joined the crowds
in the stadium and waited to cheer on
Blink and the other contestants. A group
of cheerleaders came out onto the field.
Some of them wore bandages and

 plasters and
moved very
stiffly, but the
spectators felt
sorry for
them and
clapped
anyway.

Teggs watched as the guard fiddled about inside each robo-boxer with a screwdriver. The cleaner seemed to be watching closely too.

"Sorry about the delay, folks!" Mr Edvill's voice rumbled out of the speakers. "But while we sort out a technical hitch with the robo-boxers, let's have some dino-athletics."

The crowd went wild again, cheering as a bunch of older cadets took to the field. Hidden high jumps and hurdles and all kinds of sports equipment rose up from out of the ground in between the boxing rings.

"Let's kick off with the pole vault!" cried Mr Edvill. "Our first contestant is year three cadet Zed Abee . . ."

Teggs watched as a large grey stegosaurus picked up the pole and ran towards a high bar. But the moment she stuck the pole in the ground . . . *KA-ZAMM!* It exploded! The crowd gasped as the stegosaurus was knocked over backwards. Moments later, two triceratops dashed along to help her onto a stretcher.

"What happened there?" Teggs wondered.

"Search me, dude," said Dutch, dumbfounded.

"No need to worry, folks," announced Mr Edvill. "I'm being told that Zed's accident was due to a freak build up of static electricity, and she is not badly hurt. So let's switch to Harlan Pop in the shot put!"

A spotty hadrosaur in a baseball cap ran onto the field, holding the shot – a large metal ball. With a loud grunt, he hurled it through the air . . .

But the shot came flying back at him and conked him on the head! "*Oof!*" cried Harlan Pop – and again the crowd gasped

in horror. The two triceratops hurried back with their stretcher.

"I didn't see that coming," Dutch admitted.

"Neither did Harlan!" said Teggs.

The crowd was murmuring uneasily.

"No need for alarm!" Mr Edvill insisted as the cleaning dinosaur rushed to clear away the shot before anyone else could come near. "Er . . . a freak gust of wind blew the ball back at our brave hadrosaur. But he 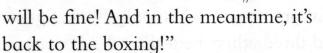 will be fine! And in the meantime, it's back to the boxing!"

The crowd clapped again, but with less enthusiasm. Even so, as Blink led the young cadets out into the stadium, Teggs and Dutch cheered as loudly as they could. Blink had a boxing glove on each wing and an extra-large one on his beak! Splatt waddled nervously behind him. With Damona and Netta not there to give support, Teggs and Dutch cheered for him too.

The contest began. Blink and Splatt battled well! Luckily, there were no more freaky accidents or red-light problems – while only Blink, Splatt and three others beat the robo-boxers, none of the losers was hurt.

"Phew!" said Mr Edvill. "Please congratulate the five winners who go through to the next round." The crowd cheered more loudly again. "We will now take a break until tomorrow morning. And don't forget, the day begins with a rock tennis tournament . . ."

As the announcements went on and the crowds drifted away, Teggs and Dutch ran to congratulate their friend.

"Did you see me, Teggs?" Blink was hopping up and down with excitement. "Did you, Dutch?"

Dutch grinned. "You were awesome, dude!"

"We beat the robots!" Splatt cheered.
"I only wish Netta had made it too.
Can we go and see her?"

"We will catch a taxi to the hospital
right away," Teggs declared.

The hospital was a large, blue dome
with a big, red cross on it, backing onto
the desert
sands. Inside,
the waiting
room was full
of injured
cadets. Teggs
saw Zed,
the grey
stegosaurus
from the pole
vault, propped up in a chair, covered in
soot. Shot-putting Harlan Pop sat beside
her with a big bump on his head.

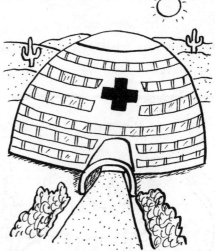

Two dinosaur cheerleaders with red
pom-poms tied to their tails and red

plasters on their heads walked stiffly
through the waiting room as if in a
daze.

"What happened to them?" Splatt
wondered.

"A whole bunch of cheerleaders hurt
themselves two days ago," said Harlan
Pop. "They were rehearsing some moves
on stage and didn't notice a puddle of
oil, spilled there by accident. They all
slipped off!"

Teggs felt worried. "I wonder if these
injuries really *are* 'accidents'," he said.

Dutch frowned. "What else would they be, dude?"

"Remember the boxing robots that just happened to go haywire?" Teggs shrugged. "Maybe someone *wants* things to go wrong around here . . ."

"Hey, there's Netta on her stretcher!" said Blink suddenly, flapping up into the air to see.

Teggs and his friends made their way through the patients to join her.

"I won!" Splatt beamed, hugging her. "Oh, and the dino-bird did OK too."

"Well done!" said Netta. "I wish I had won."

"We bought you some flowers to cheer you up," said Dutch, looking sheepish. "But they looked so tasty. we accidentally ate them!"

"Thanks!" grumped Netta.

"Where's Damona?" asked Splatt, looking round.

A piercing voice rang through the room. "My friend needs a doctor *now*!"

Dutch winced. "I think we've found her!"

Damona marched a mammoth in a green gown across the room. He was big, brown and hairy with a dribbly trunk, and a stethoscope hung from his large shoulders. He looked cross.

"Here she is, Doctor Finkle," said Damona. "Fix her up!"

"My dear diceratops," said Finkle, brushing her away with his trunk. "I am the only doctor on duty and there  are more serious cases to treat. Good day!" With that, he stomped over to Harlan Pop and led him away.

"Thanks for trying, Damona," said Netta.

Just then, Mr Edvill and Bomp entered the waiting room.

"Hello, all!" boomed Mr Edvill, looking very smart in his blue suit. "I just wanted to tell you how sorry I am for all the accidents. I'm afraid the first Megasaur Challenge has got off to a rotten start."

The injured cadets grumbled noisily.

"But here's the good news," Bomp added. "However injured you are, I have persuaded Mr Edvill to let you all stay in the competition. We will find an event you can do, even if you're in plaster from head to tail!"

A cheer went up from the cadets.

Netta bounced up and down on her stretcher. "Now *all* Damona's Darlings can take part again!" she said happily.

"Hurt dinosaurs shouldn't play sports," Blink twittered. "They should rest."

"Rubbish!" Netta snorted, still bouncing. "You're just scared because you know I could beat you with *two* sprained ankles—Whoops!" She bounced so hard that the stretcher broke and she tumbled through it onto the floor!

Dutch tried not to laugh. "How about *four* sprained ankles, Netta?"

"I think I need a doctor!" Netta groaned.

49

"Let's hope tomorrow's events go more smoothly," said Teggs. But inside he had a feeling that told him there was danger close at hand.

Only then did he notice the cleaner watching him from across the waiting room, with dark, narrowed eyes . . .

Chapter Five

TROUBLE WITH TENNIS

Although his hotel bed was made of the softest moss, Teggs  didn't sleep well that night. It wasn't Dutch's snoring that kept him awake, or Blink's fidgeting. He kept thinking of all the strange accidents – and the shifty-looking cleaner who had followed them to the hospital . . .

Was something strange going on, or was he worrying about nothing? Teggs didn't want to mention his suspicions to the others. They were having fun and he didn't want to put them off their events. But if they were in danger . . .

Finally he dozed off.

"SQUAWK!" Teggs woke with a start to find that Blink was flapping around the room with a piece of paper in his claws. "Rise and shine, everyone. It's five o'clock in the morning and I've been sorting out your timetables!"

"*Five?*" Dutch hid his head under the pillow. "Dude, *you* are the one who needs sorting out."

"Now, now!" Blink perched on Dutch's tummy and pecked away the pillow. "You have an important game of rock tennis at nine-thirty and you need to practise. It's mixed doubles. You will be playing against some year three cadets . . . with Damona."

"Oh, no," Dutch groaned. "She will be telling me what to do the whole time!"

Teggs frowned. "How do you know all this, Blink?"

"I just flew over to the stadium where they have posted the players' list," he explained. "It was lovely and quiet. The only person I saw there was the cleaner . . ."

"That cleaner gets everywhere," Teggs muttered. "What was he doing at the hospital yesterday?"

"Um, cleaning?" Dutch suggested. "With all the accidents, maybe Doctor Finkle needed extra help."

"Maybe." Teggs sighed. He was still worried. "What's my first event?"

"Weightlifting at ten-thirty," said Blink. "And I've got the javelin at midday with Netta – so long as her ankle is better." He blinked faster and faster. "Now, come on, you two. Let's get down to the training rooms. The Daring Dinos need to be in beak condition."

"That's *peak* condition," said Teggs.

Blink grinned. "Not in my case!"

While Blink flapped on ahead, Teggs and Dutch jogged sleepily to the stadium. They stopped off several times to chomp on the delicious plants growing beside the road. Soon they felt full of strength and energy and ready to train.

The time passed quickly. While Dutch practised swatting rocks with his racquet, and Blink's beak got busy hurling javelins, Teggs worked out with the dumbbells. A special robot – a robo-ball, like a massive ball with chunky arms – put the weights on the bar for him to lift. Teggs had a strong tail, and he soon found he could lift quite heavy weights.

He noticed Netta watching him from beside the robo-ball. She had a red plaster on her head. "Hi, Netta. How are you feeling?"

"The hospital was very nice," she said slowly, as if in a daze. "They made me better. Now I can throw the javelin."

"Not as well as me," cried Blink.
"Look!" He hurled a rubber spear into
a large safety net.

Netta simply turned and walked
away. "Goodbye."

"What's up with her?" said Dutch,
scratching his head.

Just then, Damona burst in wearing
her full sports kit of pink vest, shorts and
trainers with sparkly ribbons. "Right,
Dutch Delaney!" she cried. "Let's get on
that tennis court. I will hit every rock,
because I'm brilliant. You just try not to
get in the way." She fluttered her eyelids.

"Come on, then!"

Dutch sighed
and walked
out with her.
"This is
going to be
a long game!"

"Good luck." Teggs grinned. "Come
on, Blink, let's cheer them on."

Dinosaurs of all shapes and sizes were
pouring into the stadium as the two
friends made their way to their seats.
Splatt was sitting on his own.

"Have you seen Netta?" he asked. "I
thought she would want to watch."

"She *was* in the training room," said
Teggs.

Down in the arena, the boxing rings
were gone. In their place was a large
rock tennis court, the outer edges
marked with big boulders. On one side
of the vine net stood Dutch and
Damona, holding their racquets with

their tails. On the other stood a grey stegosaurus and a spotty hadrosaur wearing red plasters on their heads.

"Hey, that's Zed Abee!" Teggs realized. "The poor old stego-girl whose pole vault blew up."

"And that's Harlan Pop!" Blink bounced up and down in his seat. "He bumped his head on the shot put, remember."

"Hello, dino-ladies and gentle-saurs!" Mr Edvill's voice boomed brightly from the speakers. "Welcome to day two of the Megasaur Challenge – hopefully with no more accidents! Let's start with the first round of the mixed doubles Rock Tennis Tournament!"

The audience cheered and clapped as the players were introduced. Bomp was the umpire and sat in a big raised seat. He held up his arm and the applause died down.

"First serve to Zed and Harlan," Bomp cried.

Zed picked a rock from the pile behind her. She chucked the stone in

the air and then hit it over the net . . .

Damona ran forward and knocked the rock back. Harlan Pop whacked it towards Dutch. Dutch easily hit it back over.

But then Zed Abee socked the rock hard with her racquet. It went flying straight at Damona . . .

"Look out!" Dutch yelled.

But Damona couldn't duck in time.

BONK! The rock bounced off her
horns – and Damona fell to the
ground . . .

Chapter Six

CRASHING TO A HALT!

The crowd gasped in horror.

"Dino down!" yelled Dutch, rushing to Damona's side. "We need a stretcher!"

"Poor Damona!" cried Splatt.

"Zed did that on purpose," said Teggs hotly, and Blink nodded.

The two triceratops turned up with their stretcher. The crowd started to boo Zed Abee.

"You are disqualified!" Bomp shouted.

Two kentrosaurus security guards came on to take Zed away. She went with them as if in a daze. So did Harlan Pop. The puzzling pair reminded Teggs of Netta in the training room.

Damona got up on wobbly legs and Dutch helped her to climb onto the stretcher. She waved bravely. The audience clapped her.

"Oh, dear . . ." Mr Edvill's voice sounded strained over the speakers. "I'm afraid we must cancel the rock tennis while Damona gets checked at the hospital – escorted by her fellow cadet Dutch."

"*Another* visit to the hospital." Teggs shook his head. "This Megasaur Challenge is mega-unlucky!"

The audience of sponsors and sports fans were crossly shaking their heads. Some more bandaged-up cheerleaders were sent on.

Their injuries made them move very stiffly and slowly, the plasters on their heads as red as their pom-poms.

"This whole contest is rubbish!" one dinosaur shouted.

"I've got eggs at home that could run it better," agreed another.

"We will have the weightlifting contest in just a few minutes," said Mr Edvill hopefully. "Contestants, please report to the changing rooms!"

Blink blinked. "Good luck, Teggs."

"I think you might need it," said Splatt.

Teggs left the muttering crowd and took the contestants' tunnel to the changing rooms.

He saw Netta coming the other way, and waved. But she passed by and ignored him.

She really is in a funny mood, Teggs thought. I suppose she's heard about Damona and it's made her upset.

He trotted on to the changing rooms. He was the first one there . . . except for the cleaning dinosaur! The scaly scrubber was peering at the two weightlifting robo-balls.

"What are you up to?" Teggs demanded.

The cleaner jumped in the air. "Nothing!" he said. "I saw your friend Netta hanging out beside these robots. And when she left, I . . . I just thought I would clean them."

He hurried away. Teggs watched him
go suspiciously. "I've got my eye on
you!" he called after the cleaner. Then
he checked the robots. There was no sign
that they had been messed about with
and Teggs had to admit they were very
clean.

He got changed into his sports kit as
the other contestants arrived. Then
Bomp appeared and hurried them all
onto the field. The crowd applauded,
and Teggs felt nerves tingling in his

tummy. The
ball-shaped
robots rumbled
along behind
the contestants,
dragging the
heavy rack of
barbells with
their powerful
metal muscles.

"First up is
Teggs Stegosaur!"
announced Mr
Edvill. There was
more applause. Blink
almost clapped his wings off!

"Robots!" Bomp barked. "Pick up the
quarter-ton barbell!"

The robo-balls rolled over to the rack
full of weights. They hesitated. Then they
glowed bright red and smashed into the
rack as hard as they could! Huge
barbells and one-ton weights were sent

rumbling towards the contestants at break neck speed. . .

"*Move!*" shouted Teggs. He hurled himself at the other cadets, knocking them out of the way.

The weights rolled on, missing them by millimetres, and – *BOOM!* – smashed straight through the side of the stadium! The spectators in the seats above jumped up and scattered in a mad rush.

Security guards charged up and helped
them to safety – and just in time. No
sooner had they got clear than their
seats collapsed into a canyon of
crumbling concrete!

"That was too close," said Teggs
grimly.

The audience was in uproar! The
angry shouts came one after the other.

"We are not staying here."

"Whatever next?"

"We will *all* end up in hospital at this
rate!"

"Everyone stay calm!" Mr Edvill appealed, but he was drowned out by the thump of footsteps as the spectators stomped out. "Please don't go . . ."

But no one listened. Soon, the whole stadium was empty.

Blink flew over and landed beside Teggs. He helped the cadets get up, clucking over them like an anxious mother hen.

Bomp stared at the concrete pile-up at the side of the stadium. "I can't believe this has happened," he said miserably.

"I saw a cleaner hanging around the robots," said Teggs. "I'm sure he had something to do with them going wrong."

"I don't think so, Teggs," said Mr Edvill sadly, joining them on the field. "That cleaner came highly recommended . . ."

"It's not just the robots in any case," said Bomp. "*Everything* has gone wrong!"

"I'm afraid you are right." Mr Edvill sniffed sadly. "The stadium is not safe, and no one wants to watch our contest anyway. From this moment, the Megasaur Challenge is cancelled!"

Chapter Seven

THROUGH THE ROOF!

Teggs, Blink, Splatt and the other contestants were sent back to the hotel. Zed, Harlan and Netta went straight up to their rooms. So did the bandaged cheerleaders. The rest of the cadets sat in the lounge, feeling very down in the dumps.

The only good news came when Dutch brought Damona back from hospital with just a red plaster on her head.

"Look who's here!" he yelled.

"Welcome back!" cheered Splatt.

"Thank you," said Damona slowly. "The hospital was nice."

Teggs frowned. "Are you sure you're all right?" She seemed in a daze, just like Netta, Zed and Harlan had been.

"Doctor Finkle said everything was cool," said Dutch. "Guess her head's so thick it takes more than a rock to knock it!"

"Yes," Damona agreed, touching her plaster. "I think I shall go and see Netta now." And with that she went upstairs.

Blink hopped up to Dutch. "Did you hear about the Megasaur Challenge being cancelled?"

"I sure did." Dutch pulled a face. "The whole thing sucks."

"Indeed it does!" said Mr Edvill, stepping sadly into the hotel with Bomp at his side. "Hello, everyone. I just wanted to say a big thank you for taking part. I am sorry so many things went wrong."

Bomp nodded sadly. "We have spoken to Commander Gruff. He says that you may all stay here tonight. Then, in the morning,  astro-jets will take you back to the academy and—"

Suddenly, there was a loud crashing noise from upstairs. It sounded like a small asteroid had just crashed into the ceiling. Everyone looked up and frowned.

Bomp cleared his throat, "As I was saying—"

But then there was a louder crash – as if a slightly larger asteroid had landed upstairs.

"What's right above us?" Teggs wondered.

"Er . . ." Blink thought hard. "I think it's Damona's room!"

"I hope she's all right," said Splatt.

There came another crash, and another — as if lots of different asteroids were hitting one after the other, getting bigger each time.

BOOM! A big crack opened up in the ceiling. Plaster dust filled the room like smoke.

"Oh, no!" cried Mr Edvill. "Now what?"

"Everyone out!" roared Teggs. As the crashes kept on coming, he shooed the other cadets out of the room. "Dutch, Blink — help me!"

Dutch grabbed Bomp and Mr Edvill
and dragged them away. Blink flew
ahead and opened the main doors
so everyone could run outside safely.
But then Teggs saw a hotel dino-maid
cowering in the corner. *BOOOOM!* The
biggest bang yet rocked the room, and
the ceiling split right open.
Something began to
push through . . .

"Quick!"
gasped
Teggs. He
hooked his
tail under
the maid's
apron
strings and
lifted her up,
then hurled
her across
the room to
safety . . .

As a *bed* came crashing through from upstairs!

Teggs just had time to see that Damona, Netta, Zed, Harlan and several cheerleaders were all bouncing up and down on the giant mattress. Then it smashed to the floor close beside him in a shower of rubble! Damona and the others had a soft landing on the squashy

PLEASE
DO NOT
BREAK
ANYTHING

bedsprings – but a huge piece of plaster crashed down on Teggs's spiky back.

"Ooof!" he gasped.

Dutch and Blink came rushing back inside with Bomp – and stopped dead in astonishment.

Blink blinked so fast he whipped up a minor dust storm! "What's going on here?"

Damona groaned, looking around in a daze.

"We were bouncing on the bed," said Netta slowly. Zed nodded, touching the red plaster on her head. "We must have jumped too hard."

"Yes, it was an accident," added a cross-eyed cheerleader. But she didn't sound as if she was sorry or upset or anything at all.

Dutch crouched besides Teggs. "Are you OK?"

"I think so," said Teggs weakly.

"I'll call for a stretcher," said Bomp. "I've had a lot of practice lately!"

Blink hopped over to Teggs and patted him on the shoulder. "Dutch and I will wait with you."

"No," said Teggs. He pointed up at the huge jagged hole in the ceiling. "I'm OK. Go and get *him*."

Blink and Dutch looked up – to find the mysterious cleaner looking down at them through the hole. Realizing he had been spotted, the cleaner ran away . . . Dutch galloped over to the stairs. "Come on, Blink. Teggs is right – that dude has some explaining to do!"

Damona and the other dazed dinosaurs seemed unhurt by their fall, so only Teggs had to go to the hospital. Bomp went with him in the flying taxi. When they arrived the waiting room was dark and deserted.

"I don't care what Mr Edvill says," Teggs muttered. "I'm sure that cleaner has something to do with all this. He keeps turning up whenever there's an accident."

"Forget him," said Bomp. "You have more important things to worry about . . ."

Suddenly, a scruffy, hairy, dribbly mammoth appeared. It was Dr Finkle. He looked at Teggs and frowned. "Is he

the only one who was hurt? I was
expecting lots more."

"So was I!" Bomp glared at Teggs.
"This troublesome stego-twit got
everyone to safety. He keeps mucking up
our plans."

"Your plans?" Teggs tried to get up
from his stretcher.
But Bomp
held him down.
"What are you
on about?
Let me go!"

"Oh, we will
certainly let
you go," said
Finkle. "Once we
have turned you
into our secret slave!"

Teggs gulped. "*What?*"

"It is time you learned my secret," said
Finkle. Smiling, he untucked a hairy flap
of rubber from the neck of his doctor's

overalls and pulled. His face was just a
mask! Underneath was a smaller head –
green and scaly with fierce little eyes
and rows of rotten teeth like yellow
icicles. He struggled out of his huge,
hairy costume to reveal small arms on
a massive, powerful body.

"You aren't a mammoth!" Teggs gasped. "You are a meat-eater in disguise!"

"That's right, you plant-eating potato!" hissed Finkle, rubbing his claws together. "I am a *carnotaur* – and you are my prisoner!"

Chapter Eight

SLAVES OF THE CARNOTAUR

Teggs tried to stay cool, but it wasn't easy. The carnotaur's breath stank of raw meat and his dribble was yellow, like cooking oil. Bomp's heavy front legs were pinning Teggs to the stretcher so he couldn't turn away.

"I've been wrong all along," Teggs groaned. "It wasn't the cleaner making all those accidents happen. It was *you*, Bomp!"

"That's right," Bomp agreed. "I slipped up the cheerleaders, messed up the robo-boxers, mucked up the shot put and *blew* up the pole vault!" He sniggered. "I am working for Doctor Finkle."

"But why?" Teggs cried. "He is a meat-eating menace! With *very* smelly breath."

"He is also very rich," said Bomp. "I am poor. A triceratops trainer gets paid peanuts. Pah! I don't even *like* peanuts!"

"Bomp prefers gold," hissed Finkle. "So I paid him to sneak me into the sports village from outer space and cause all these accidents."

"Why?" Teggs glared at the carnotaur. "What are you up to, tooth-chops?"

"I am changing the minds of my patients!" Finkle held up a small square of red sticking plaster in his little claws. "Hidden in my plasters are clever little devices. Once the controls are set here in the hospital, they block brainwaves and stop you thinking for yourself." He grinned and dribbled. "Once one of my special plasters is stuck to your skin you will do whatever I tell you!"

"So that's why Damona, Netta, Zed and all the others were acting so strangely," said Teggs. "Those red plasters have turned them into your slaves!"

"That's right," Bomp agreed. "We told Zed to hit the rock at Damona and told Netta to muck up the weightlifting robots."

Teggs nodded. "Because every time someone got hurt they were brought here to the hospital . . . so you could turn them into slaves too."

"Correct," snarled Finkle. "Tomorrow, the astro-jets will come to take all cadets back to Astrosaurs Academy. But the cadets will be under *my* control." He chuckled, enjoying the moment. "The oldest ones will leave soon to join the DSS. They will be my secret spies!"

"And what about the youngest cadets like me?" asked Teggs.

"At my command, you and your friends will *destroy* Astrosaurs Academy!" Finkle chuckled. "Then the DSS will have no new astrosaurs — and my spies will destroy all the existing ones!"

Teggs groaned. "Meaning meat-eaters can invade plant-eater planets 'without a care."

"And meaning *I* will be rich enough to buy a world of my own," said Bomp. "I shall make Mr Edvill work for me – as *my* slave. HA!"

"But your plans are spoiled now, remember?" said Teggs. "The Megasaur Challenge is cancelled so you can't cause any more 'accidents' in the arena. And I was the only one hurt when the bed came through the ceiling at the  hotel." Teggs smiled with satisfaction. "No one else will come to this hospital – so you can't take over their brains!"

"I can if I cause *more* accidents," said Finkle nastily. "Bomp – activate plan R."

Teggs frowned. "Plan R?"

"A plan I had up my sleeve in case anyone escaped the crashing bed." Finkle grinned. "Plan R – for *Robot*."

Bomp pressed a button on his remote control. Suddenly, Teggs heard a clanking noise start up just outside. A moment later, robo-boxers and robo-balls came crashing and rumbling into the waiting room! They pushed past Teggs, Bomp and Finkle. Big boxing gloves punched the air on long steel tentacles. Massive arms shoved chairs and tables aside as the menacing metal monsters moved towards the main doors.

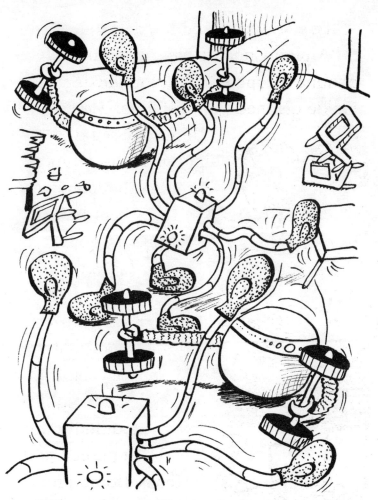

"The robots will attack the Ferns Hotel," said Bomp. "What a lot of accidents they will cause . . ."

"But people could be badly hurt!" Teggs shouted.

"Oooh, yes," hissed Finkle. He leaned over Teggs with the little red plaster. "Your friends will *have* to come here, Teggs. Like you, they will become my slaves!"

"Do you want to bet on that, dude?" came a familiar voice from the main doorway.

"Dutch!" Teggs beamed.

The diplodocus winked. "Large as life and ready for action!"

"Fool!" Finkle shouted. "These robots shall squish you."

"Not if we have anything to do with it!" Blink yelled, flapping into the room with a pile of javelins. "Now all the Daring Dinos are together!" He started

to hurl the pointed poles down at the robots like an expert athlete.

CLANG – *BZZZZZZ!* The javelins stuck into the robots like pins in a pincushion, scrambling their circuits.

"No!" cried Bomp.

"Yes!" cheered Teggs. "Good work, Blink."

Blink winked at him. "All my javelin practice wasn't wasted after all!"

The robo-boxers began to beat up the robo-balls. The robo-balls glowed red and ran over the robo-boxers. Dutch joined in, pushing and pounding his way through the mashed-up metal, trying to get to Teggs. It was complete carnage!

"Hold it, both of you!" Bomp shouted, tightening his grip on Teggs. "Or Finkle will *eat* your friend."

But the next moment, an out-of-control robo-boxer punched Bomp with seven boxing gloves. "Oof!" yelled the triceratops. He was knocked flying and landed in a dazed heap.

"Free!" Teggs cried. He sat up and knocked the red plaster from Finkle's little hands. "Careful, butter-claws!"

Angrily, Finkle opened his jaws and lunged for Teggs. But Teggs rolled away just in time, and all the carnotaur got was a mouthful of metal stretcher and some broken teeth! "Oww!" cried the carnotaur, falling to the floor.

"How do you like it when accidents happen to you?" Teggs cried. Dutch and Blink pushed through the last of the half-wrecked robots to stand by his side.

"You are beaten, Finkle. Give up and come quietly."

"Never!" the meat-eater roared. He jumped up and slapped Teggs, Dutch and Blink on the head with his little claws. Then he backed away.

"Is that the best you can do?" sneered Dutch.

Finkle smiled. "I think it will do!"

Suddenly, Teggs realized what the carnotaur had done. "The red plasters," he gasped. "He's stuck them on us!" Already, Teggs could feel his mind turning hazy. "It's . . . getting . . . hard . . . to think . . ."

Dutch and Blink were already staring into space with googly eyes.

"I told you I would make you my slaves," hissed Finkle. "Nothing can stop my plans. *Nothing!*"

Chapter Nine

CLEANING UP!

"*We* can stop you!" boomed a stranger's voice from the doorway.

Using all his concentration, Teggs turned to see who was talking.

It was the cleaner!

The cleaner squirted gallons of gloopy liquid soap at Dr Finkle's feet.

"Whoops!" The carnotaur slipped over and crashed to the ground. He tried to get up again, but now he was covered in soap and suds. "Help!" he bawled, spitting out soap as he slithered helplessly on his back.

"I'm stuck!"

"And you'll stay that way!" shouted Damona, charging into the waiting room. Netta, Splatt, Zed Abee and Harlan Pop were just behind her! She ran up to Teggs and pulled off the plaster from his head. Netta and Zed did the same for Dutch and Blink, while Harlan and Splatt ran over to Bomp and Finkle with some handcuffs.

"Damona!" Teggs spluttered. "Are you back to normal?"

She grinned. "I think you will find I'm better than ever!"

"We all are," said Netta, patting Dutch and Blink on the back. "Thanks to the cleaner!"

The cleaner crossed to them, a big smile on his face. "Well done, guys. You solved the mystery of the deliberate accidents before I did."

"Only by mistake." Teggs looked sheepish. "I thought you were behind everything."

"And it's a good job you did," said Blink. "Dutch and I caught the cleaner at the hotel like you told us to – but then he *came* clean."

"Turns out this dude's not really a cleaner at all," Dutch added. "He's an *astrosaur* – working undercover!"

"*That* is why he turned up everywhere!" Netta cried.

"I'm a friend of Commander Gruff," the cleaner admitted. "The name is Sergeant Snoop. Mr Edvill was worried when the cheerleaders slipped in that oil, in case someone left it there on purpose. So Gruff sent me along to check it out."

"Bomp did it," said Teggs, as the triceratops started to stir. "Every accident brought more patients for Finkle to make into slaves with his red plasters."

"But when I fell through the ceiling, my plaster came off!" said Damona. "I could think for myself again — and I remembered what happened here."

"So we all rushed over," Dutch added.

"I'm glad you did," said Teggs. "But how come you and Blink got here ahead of everyone else?"

Blink blinked. "Because you are our best friend, of course!"

"Team hug!" Dutch cried, and Teggs happily hugged them both.

"You puny plant-eaters," Finkle wailed, still sliding helplessly about on his back.

"My plan nearly worked!"

"And I was almost rich!" grouched Bomp, sulking in his handcuffs.

"And now you will both *certainly* go to prison!" said Mr Edvill, poking his long neck through the doors. "My security guards will lock you up until some astrosaurs come to take you away."

"Bah!" Finkle grumbled. "Not fair."

Dutch smiled. "Someone should stick a plaster over his mouth."

"I wish someone could simply stick a plaster on my stadium and make it better," said Mr Edvill. "Thanks to this rotten pair, the Megasaur Challenge has been a total disaster. I doubt there will ever be another."

"But now you can start *this* one all over again," said Teggs. "It will be perfectly safe."

"No more accidents," Netta said happily.

Blink nodded. "Maybe Commander Gruff will let us help you repair the arena."

"Yes," said Damona. "After all, we came here for a contest – and a contest is what we want!"

"Too right," Dutch cried, and the others all agreed.

"You really do want to help?" Mr Edvill smiled. "You are *all* Megasaurs!"

"You're right there," said Sergeant Snoop. "And I will make sure Commander Gruff knows it. I will suggest that he gives you all a special medal for what you've done today!"

Teggs and his friends glowed with pride.

"Come on, then," said Blink, blinking

away. "Let's get to the stadium!"

Teggs nodded. "I bet if we all work together we can get it fixed before too many sponsors and spectators leave. Because at the end of the day we are one big winning team . . ."

He grinned. "Astrosaurs Academy United!"

"UNITED!" boomed the other cadets. And as Mr Edvill's security guards took Bomp and Finkle away, Teggs and his friends went off to work . . . So they could play!

THE END

ASTROSAURS ACADEMY
DESTINATION DANGER!
STEVE COLE

Young Teggs stegosaur is a pupil at **ASTROSAURS ACADEMY** – where dinosaurs train to be **ASTROSAURS!** With his best friends Blink and Dutch beside him, amazing adventures and far-out-fun are never far away!

Teggs and his fellow astro-cadets Arriving at the academy, the new astro-cadets face their first mission – to camp out in a deserted space wilderness and bring back something exciting for show-and-tell. But the sneaky tricks of a rival team mean big trouble for Teggs, Blink and Dutch – especially when a T. rex ship crash-lands close by with a VERY hungry crew . . .

ISBN: 978 1 862 30555 7

Astrosaurs

THE SUN-SNATCHERS
STEVE COLE

Teggs is no ordinary
dinosaur - he's an
ASTROSAUR!
Captain of the
amazing spaceship DSS *Sauropod*,
he goes on dangerous missions and
fights evil - along with his faithful
crew, Gipsy, Arx and Iggy!

A world of woolly rhinos is
in desperate peril - one of their three
suns has gone missing! Racing to the
rescue, Teggs and his team must fight
a gigantic star-swallowing menace
before theother two suns get snatched
away. And all the time, other
dangers are drawing closer . . .

ISBN: 978 1 862 30254 9